Lola Koala and the
Ten Times Worse Than Anything

Lola Koala and the
Ten Times Worse Than Anything

Muriel Blaustein

Harper & Row, Publishers

To little sisters…to big sisters

Lola Koala and the Ten Times Worse Than Anything
Copyright © 1987 by Muriel Blaustein
Printed in Singapore. All rights reserved.

Library of Congress Cataloging-in-Publication Data
Blaustein, Muriel.
    Lola Koala and the ten times worse than anything.

    Summary: Two sisters realize they can be brave about
different things when Lola, the younger, is timid about
scary movies and high places and her big sister is
terrified of the amusement park rides.

    [1. Sisters—Fiction.   2. Fear—Fiction]   I. Title.
PZ7.B61625Lo 1987   [E]   86-22811
ISBN 0-694-00220-8
ISBN 0-06-020539-3 (lib. bdg.)

1 2 3 4 5 6 7 8 9 10
First Edition

Lola Koala and her Big Sis spent a week
every summer with their Grandma.
"The new amusement park has just opened.

We can go tomorrow," said Grandma.

The next day it rained,
and Lola was glad.

Grandma drove them
to the movies instead.

She bought them tickets and popcorn.

But Lola hid under the seat. The movies were scary.

Sis said, "Honestly, Lola! This is only a movie."

The next morning was hot,
and they went to the pool.

Lola walked to the edge of the diving board.

Sis had to come and get her.

The day after that, they went for a quiet drive.

But the high, curving road made Lola sick.

Grandma had to pull over.

"Well, tomorrow we go to the amusement park," Sis said.

HOW COME YOU'RE SO BRAVE, SIS?

BIG SISTERS ARE JUST BRAVER THAN LITTLE SISTERS

"Was it true?" Lola wondered. She could hardly sleep.

Grandma bought them tickets for all the rides.

Lola was worried.

But Sis said, "We'll just go on the easy ones."

But Lola and Sis rode into the tunnel…

of horrors!

Sis held Lola tightly.

Lola thought, "The creature feature was worse!"

Lola wanted to try the Ferris wheel.

Sis tried to talk her out of it.

They floated on seats high up in the sky.
"This isn't even wobbly," thought Lola.
"Why, the edge of the diving board was worse!"

Sis covered her eyes and didn't dare look.

Lola and Sis couldn't figure it out.

Grandma was waiting for them.

Grandma decided to join them on their next ride...

Slowly, cranking and grinding, they rose

higher and higher to the top. Lola thought,

"The drive in the mountains was ten times worse!"

Grandma had to take Sis to the washroom, but Lola felt great.

That night, Sis said, "How come you weren't scared?"

"Well," Lola said, "I think…

big and little sisters can be brave about different things."

And she was right.